HINNOM MAGAZINE

"A journal of
certainly delive
ries which fo
ringly abnorı
way where yc
    don't want ...

peeled for the next issue."—Kev Harrison,
        THIS IS HORROR

"In Hinnom Magazine, C. P. Dunphey is
quietly pulling together a collection of stories
and authors that stands the best chance of
being the spiritual successor to 'Weird Tales'
available to this new generation of readers."—Ryan Whitley, THE MISKATONIC
        REVIEW

THE WORLD'S MOST POPULAR MAG-
AZINE OF WEIRD FICTION & COSMIC
HORROR

HINNOM

MAGAZINE

SPRING 2019/ ISSUE 010

EDITED BY C. P. DUNPHEY &
CALEB STEPHENS

GEHENNA & HINNOM BOOKS

Gehennabooks.com

Copyright © 2019 by Gehenna & Hinnom Books
ISBN: 978-1-950642-00-7

Printed in the United States of America
Cover Illustration by Dave Dick
All Rights Reserved

TABLE OF CONTENTS:

INTRODUCTION:
WE'RE BACK
C. P. DUNPHEY

It feels good to be back. I want to immediately thank everyone reading this, and all the individuals who have read the magazines in the past. Your patience during the past several months has been more appreciated than you may ever know. I suppose a quick recap is in order for those of you who may be new readers or new to the company in general. We had a massively successful Kickstarter in the beginning of the year. Thanks to a large number of amazing backers, we raised over $10,000, smashing our initial goal of $3,000. What does this mean? Well, it means that Gehenna & Hinnom has a massive docket of releases scheduled for 2019. This includes several collections, anthologies, magazines (like the one you're reading), and more. We've also become a professional paying market due to the massive contributions to the crowdfunding campaign. For those of you who have been following along since this all began, you'll know my singular dream has always been to make *Hinnom Magazine* a professional paying market, so one more check off the bucket list.

Why would I want *Hinnom* to become a professional paying market, you ask? Because authors should be able to live off their work. This is the first major step in our march towards helping authors find success. Now, there will be challenges. Many. A lot of literary projects just aren't profitable for publishers, hence why major magazines like *Apex* close their doors. To combat this, we have to be smart, as the last thing we'd ever want is to be another market that has shut down due to an unsustainable business structure.

You may be wondering why I'm bringing all this up. The reason is that we are going to release several collections and anthologies before the next issue of the magazine comes out. The reason being is that we have to make sure to bank a profit before the budget dries up, which the magazine could do very quickly. So, expect to see several other releases before *Hinnom 011*, but we do have the next five issues already planned. Stories have already been accepted and artwork contracted; we just need to ensure G&H is intelligent in its approach, to avoid any delays!

So, what will the next several months have in store?

Well, *Strange Company and Others*, Peter Rawlik's debut collection, is releasing on June 15th, 2019, then S. L. Edwards's debut collection *Whiskey and Other Unusual Ghosts* is releasing in July, John S. McFarland's collection *The Dark Walk Forward and Other Stories* shortly following in August. July will also see the release of Curtis M. Lawson and Doug Rinaldi's novella *Those Who Go Forth Into the Empty Place of Gods*, and somewhere in there, we will have two anthologies: *Dark Glades and Starwinds: The Very Best of Gehenna & Hinnom Volume 1*, and *Year's Best Cosmic Horror 2019 Anthology*. We are also planning on releasing one of the chapbooks and a novelette or two in there as well (so many releases!).

Big things are on the horizon. We couldn't be more thankful for everyone who reads these stories and all the wonderful people who contributed to the Kickstarter. None of this would've been possible without you.

On a final note, we lost two important authors since the last issue. I wanted to take a moment to honor them. We will be doing much more to honor them in the future, but it wouldn't feel right not to mention them here.

W. H. Pugmire passed away after a battle with pneumonia. S. T. Joshi once told me Wilum was the author whose work closest resembled Lovecraft's, and that likely there wouldn't be another of his talent for many decades. We salute Wilum for his contributions and hope that he can finally meet Lovecraft. We know they'll have a lot to talk about now that they can finally converse.

Jeff C. Stevenson passed away after a battle with pancreatic cancer. Jeff was a hidden talent, one of the few authors I've come across who really deserved more recognition. His work has been published everywhere, and one of his stories will be appearing in an upcoming chapbook from Gehenna & Hinnom. More on that soon.

Alas, thank you for purchasing this tome. I hope you enjoy, and welcome back to the Ether.

DANCING WITH A WEREWOLF IN THE PALE MOONLIGHT:
AN EXCLUSIVE INTERVIEW WITH MAX BOOTH III

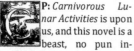**P:** *Carnivorous Lunar Activities* is upon us, and this novel is a beast, no pun intended. For our readers who may be new to your work, can you tell us a little about yourself?

MB: Sure thing. I grew up in Northern Indiana and now live in a small town outside San Antonio. I work the night shift at a hotel and write books about unlikable people doing unlikable things. I'm the co-founder and Editor-in-Chief of Perpetual Motion Machine, the Managing Editor of *Dark Moon Digest*, and the co-host of Castle Rock Radio: A Stephen King Podcast. I used to despise pickles but over the last few years I've grown to tolerate them. Mustard is my favorite condiment. I hate Jimmy Fallon.

CP: We've read about the origins of the idea for this novel and how it came to fruition, but what can you tell us about the process of writing the novel? Were there any unexpected challenges you encountered?

MB: With the first draft, I challenged myself by writing only the dialogue, then on future drafts going back and adding in the rest of the prose. This actually turned out being a lot smoother than I anticipated. However, the novel really is one long conversation, and I've had to rewrite this same conversation several times now, with each new round of edits, so after so long there came a point when I truly could not stand to hear these fucking idiots say another word.

CP: The voice in this novel is astounding, and it's so fast-paced that it's impossible to put down once picked up. Was it difficult writing a dialogue-driven narrative? Were there any dichotomies between Ted and Justin you had in mind while writing these conversations?

MB: I think Justin is definitely more vulgar than Ted. Justin also never grew up. Never got a real job. He's still living in his parents' house. The kinda guy who thinks dogfighting is cool. Ted, on the other hand, tried to mature. He got a wife, a job, a house. Except, of course, he fucked everything up and possibly lost all three. The more the story progresses, the more we realize maybe Ted's been lying to himself, and him and Justin aren't that different after all. It's not the easiest task, escaping your home town. Somehow it always finds you in the end.

CP: What challenges did you face with the task of crafting a unique spin on the werewolf genre? Any inspirations along the way that helped form your vision?

MB: Often, in horror fiction, the characters operate as if they exist in a world that does not contain horror movies. They act as if they don't already have decades of horror literature and films to use as research. So, in my novel, Justin isn't quite sure what is happening with him, but he's using his history of horror movies to make educated guesses. There is no established mythos in this book. Nobody knows shit. It's all just a big "well, maybe this will work but probably not". You see a similar mindset in David Wong's *John Dies at the End,* I think.

CP: Staying on the topic of monster movies and horror literature, why Werewolves? Did you have a pre-existing preference for Lycans?

MB: It's a lot of fun, I think, comparing werewolves to alcoholics. In both cases, the victim tends to black out, commit terrible deeds, and is forced to deal with these consequences once they wake up. Accounting for lost time is always scary, to me, and what's scarier than the possibility of having murdered a whole bunch of people?

CP: We've seen that on the way to the book launch, you were in an accident. Very happy to see you came out *mostly* unharmed. How did the reading go after that? Did the experience give you some extra adrenaline for the event?

MB: Turns out I had a concussion from the accident, which I wouldn't learn until taking a trip to the ER the next day. I was also drenched in Diet Coke during the event, which was rather unpleasant. I think the book launch went well, over all. My head was pounding before it started but seemed to go away once everything kicked into gear. Toward the end of the night, I couldn't fucking stand the pain, but at least the adrenaline managed to get me through the book launch. I'm typing up these answers exactly one week after the accident (which totaled my vehicle), and the headache is finally down to just a dull ache.

CP: A little question for the movie fans. What is your favorite Werewolf movie and/or book? Why? Did it/they lend inspiration for your novel in any way?

MB: My favorite werewolf film would have to be *Ginger Snaps,* with my favorite book being *Mongrels* by Stephen Graham Jones. I'm a sucker for coming-to-age stories and both of these handle the topic with gusto.

10

CP: What, in your own words, is the major theme(s) in *Carnivorous Lunar Activities*?

MB: Friendship, nostalgia, alcoholism, and dick jokes.

CP: Are there any more works on the horizon that our readers can look forward to from you? What's in store for Max Booth III?

MB: Well, I have a new novel I'm shopping around currently, but nothing I can really say about it yet. I'm also doing a serial novel on Patreon titled *The Geezer*. It's a weird little Christmas horror book about a family trying to kill Santa Claus. People can follow along here.

CP: We always like to end our interviews with a question for the authors out there. If you could give one tidbit of advice to an aspiring writer, what would it be?

MB: Don't get into a car accident on your way to a book launch. It really sucks.

ITS EYES ARE OPEN
BEN THOMAS

t 3:17 a.m. on June 20, 2015, American anthropologist Jared Millar leaped from the window of his tenth-story studio in downtown Kuala Lumpur. He died on impact. The screams of street-cleaning crews alerted the local *polis*, who quickly removed the shattered body and launched an investigation.

One of the detectives' first discoveries was that Millar had been alone in his studio at the time of his suicide. The apartment's sturdy oak door was bolted from the inside, and detectives found no sign of a struggle in the mess of scribbled notes, pens, research papers, liquor bottles and books scattered across the room's many desks, as well as its stone floor.

Three key details, however, raised immediate suspicion.

First, the majority of Millar's journal notes were written in an unfamiliar language—neither English, French, nor Malay. This was the reason I was called in as a consultant on the case, as I will explain in a moment.

Second, a total of thirty-four containers of various pharmaceuticals were found throughout the apartment, ranging from mild sedatives to prescription sleeping pills and narcotics, to an empty bottle of injectable surgical anesthetic, along with small amounts of stimulants such as street-grade cocaine and methamphetamine. The autopsy showed that Millar's bloodstream contained significant concentrations of these substances when he leaped from the window.

Third, Millar's eyes had been destroyed by repeated strikes from a sharp object which was quickly determined to be a shard of glass from the broken window. The autopsy concluded these wounds to be self-inflicted.

 was contacted by the Kuala Lumpur *polis* via my Universiti Kuala Lumpur email address in the middle of a busy semester to help identify and, if possible, translate the language Millar had used in his notes. At the time I knew nothing of the case itself or of Millar, or his relationship with the French-born anthropologist Elisa Fournier, whose work would prove instrumental in my understanding of certain aspects of the translation.

In the initial email, I was simply informed:

"Our detectives believe that the language of the notes is an indigenous Austronesian tribal dialect. We hope you will bring your expertise to bear on the translation. These notes serve as crucial evidence in an ongoing investigation, and a rapid response will be very much appreciated."

I politely declined, citing my heavy course load, and sent the *polis* a short list of contact emails for some of my colleagues.

Still, I couldn't help opening the first attachment and scanning Millar's lines of tight handwriting.

Had I happened to open any other attachment, or to scan any other line, I might never have taken on the assignment and I'd have no need to write this statement.

As it happened, though, I scanned a line which I immediately translated:

"Its eyes are always open."

recognized the language of Millar's notes immediately: Malagasy, the indigenous language of Madagascar, distantly related to Malay and Indonesian, but rarely heard in Malaysia, or anywhere outside the island.

As it happened, I'd backpacked through Madagascar in my grad-school years and a fair amount of my Malagasy had stuck with me. Something about that line of Millar's notes pulled at a dim memory in me; a certain story a Sakalava fisherman had whispered to me one night.

"Long ago," that fisherman told me, "a man was condemned to death for his crimes and escaped into the forest."

We were sitting on the beach on the island's western coast beneath the stars, in the light of a flickering fire. I sipped at a beer, staring into the flames, doing my best to follow the words the fisherman spoke in Malagasy-accented French, all hard-rolling r's and throaty o's.

He continued: "The criminal climbed into the trees and concealed himself from his pursuers. And when the men of the village came to that place, they found only a lemur—the indri, which is also called babakoto; the lemur who stands as tall as a man. His wide eyes shone in the twilight as he stared down at them from its perch on a high branch."

The fisherman paused, and when I looked up from the flames, he was staring into my eyes, his own eyes wide and round. In any other circumstance, it would've been a comical sight; but here by firelight, in the midst of this tale, his eyes reminded me of the great round eyes of the lemurs I'd seen along the edges of the forest. Gangly long-limbed creatures, whose round eyes with their black pinprick pupils seemed to harbor their own kind of strange, fierce intellect.

"The indri fathered all the races of lemurs," the man went on, returning his gaze to the flames. "Not only the maky with their long-striped tails, but also the red-bellied kirioka, and all the others. And some, cursed by evil spirits, gave birth to the aye-aye, who brings death."

A chill ran through me at the matter-of-fact tone with which he spoke those words. I'd heard many tales of the aye-aye in my travels across the island. The scraggly black lemurs were known for boldly sauntering into villages at dusk, eyeing the locals and sniffing their feet. In one Merina village I'd even seen a captive specimen; a creature that looked something like a cross between a monkey and a large-eared bat. It emerged in the evenings to clamber up the trees and tap their trunks with the nail of its long, bony middle finger, in search of grubs.

"When an aye-aye fixes you with its wide-eyed stare," the fisherman said, "and points the claw of its long finger at you, that means you are a marked man. You will see the aye-aye in your dreams, and you will fear to go to sleep, because you will always see it, watching you. Soon you will see it everywhere. You will go mad, and within a month you will be dead. This is why my people always kill an aye-aye on sight."

I sipped my beer, unsure of what to make of this strange story. After a moment, I saw that he wanted to add more, but was hesitant to go on. I encouraged him to tell the rest, and—after a nervous glance into the shadows around the fire—he told me one more thing.

"The aye-ayes we see near the villages are small creatures. Not much bigger than cats. But deep in the forest live aye-ayes as tall as a man, with long arms that can reach down from the branches of tall trees."

His breathing was quickening, and he cast furtive looks toward the edge of the jungle. "Those aye-ayes do not like to be seen," he told me. "If you catch sight of one by accident, it will wait until you fall asleep

that night. Then it will find you. It will reach down from among the branches, slow and silent; and with the nail of its long, thin finger, it will pierce you."

He fell silent; and when I drank another swig of my beer, I found that my mouth had gone dry. Even here, on the firelit beach, the rustle of leaves on the jungle's distant tree-line seemed to whisper secrets better not known.

"It is wisest," the fisherman said after a time, "not to walk in the forest at night."

I'd spent that night in a motel room with all the fluorescents on, slipping between sleep and half-wakefulness in an alcoholic haze, tangled among the sweaty sheets. In my dreams I feared to turn around, always expecting to find a pair of wide, round eyes watching me. And each time I awoke, I dreaded to open my eyes, for fear of what I'd find staring back.

'm still not sure why I agreed to translate Millar's journal. If someone forced me to put the urge into words, I might say I've always had a bit of a perverse bent: the more repulsed I feel by a thing, the more urgently I feel myself drawn to it; to know its source and feel it as clearly as possible. To look into its eyes.

The Kuala Lumpur *polis* quickly replied to my request for the rest of the journal. A few minutes later, I was printing off sheet after sheet of black-and-white scans of Millar's notebook pages packed with the neat, rounded letters of his handwriting.

Millar's journals began as a typical travelogue. His plane had landed in Antananarivo on May 10th. He'd spent a few days at the city's Université, meeting with Malagasy linguist Armand Rafaralahy, who was a specialist in tribal dialects of the island's interior, as well as anthropologist Elisa Fournier, whose work on Malagasy animist practices is well-known in the field.

Reading Millar's notes, I discerned that Fournier and Rafaralahy had invited him to Madagascar to conduct the sort of investigation every anthropologist dreams of:

5/15/15

Discussed logistics of traveling to the village, 80km inside Forest S9: some dirt trails, but terrain largely mountainous. SUVs can get us within 20km, but after that we'll be on foot. But I've come this far. Planning this for years.

5/17/15

Discussed research program over lunch. Rafaralahy says phonemes and grammatical features of tribe's language likely pre-date arrival of Malay speakers by 1000+ years. Extremely archaic layers of language and indigenous culture. Entirely isolated; uncontacted until just last year.

5/18/15

Talked about village's unique culture with Fournier. Society preserves highly archaic traits not only in language and genetics, but also in myth. Primate worshippers. Venerate the aye-aye as psychopomp and dreamking.

By the end of the week, the three researchers had completed their preparations. They bundled a week's worth of supplies into Rafaralahy's Toyota SUV and headed north from Antananarivo, keeping to the paved highways until they reached the edge of the jungle where paving gave way to gravelly tracks, then to pot-holed dirt trails strewn with rocks and fallen baobab trees.

Their plan was to hike twenty kilometers the first afternoon, then pitch camp at the base of the mountain where the tribe's village was located and complete the climb in the morning.

Millar's notes make it clear that they reached the campsite without incident, pitched their tents, ate a supper of beans, rice and fish heated over the fire, and headed to bed shortly after sunset.

After that, Millar's journal abruptly cuts off. When it picks up again, his neat, densely packed handwriting has been replaced with a shakier scrawl—albeit in a hand still recognizably his.

The next entry, scribbled in Millar's new hand three days later, reads as follows:

5/20/18

Villagers have bandaged my eye and applied an herbal paste. Bleeding has stopped, finally. No one here speaks a word of Malagasy or French. Still no sign of Fournier or Rafaralahy. They feed me rice three times a day, along with a meat whose source I do not know. They will not tell me what the meat is, or else they do not understand my questions.

I am not restrained, but somehow I can't bring myself to leave. I don't know why. Perhaps I fear the jungle—and to meet... no, I won't write about that. Perhaps I simply want answers. In any case, my eye is still bandaged. I will stay here a few more days, at least.

It took me some time to piece together what took place between Millar's journey to the jungle, and the days when he began taking these scattered notes in the tribe's village. I very much wish I wasn't able to make sense of what happened in that interim—but I fear that I have.

illar's journal entries are sparse and hurried for the next few weeks. After six days in the village, he somehow convinced two local men to accompany him back through the jungle, where they showed him the road that led back to the campsite.

By astonishing luck, he found Rafaralahy's keys in his tent, although there was no sign of the linguist himself; or of Fournier. When Millar questioned the village men about his colleagues, they indicated that they did not understand, or were unwilling to speak and vanished back into the jungle.

Following the dirt trail, Millar made his way back to Rafaralahy's SUV, which—again, by sheer stroke of luck—had not been discovered and stripped for parts, as abandoned vehicles so often are in rural Madagascar. The SUV's tank held enough gas to carry him back to Antananarivo, where he checked into the best expat clinic he could find and got proper antibiotic treatment for his wounded eye.

The local police questioned Millar closely, of course; and he spent the next several days chained to his hospital bed, prime suspect in his colleagues' disappearances. But either his alibi and evidence proved convincing, or the *polis* simply got tired of investigating, because a week later they packed him on a plane to Kuala

Lumpur and told him never to come back to Madagascar.

His university's reaction to his sudden empty-handed return can be gleaned from local news articles and blog posts published that week. Millar was declared to have suffered a "break from reality" in Madagascar, brought on by "work and travel stress." He was placed on a temporary administrative leave with no clear end date—in other words, suspended until someone could make sense of what had happened in Forest S9.

But Fournier and Rafaralahy were never found, and Millar's mental state continued to deteriorate. That much is clear from his journal entries over the next week:

6/3/15

Slept less than 3 hours last night. Less than 10 hours all week. Every time I close my eyes, I see It. I hear the forest, and the sounds in the dark. And I see Rafaralahy and Fournier like they were, lying under the trees, as It came down from the branches. Nothing should move like that. Down from the tree, like film unspooling in reverse. The way It reached for them. And then It turned and looked at me. Right at me.

6/5/15

Couldn't stand it—got a prescription for Ambien. Knocked me out all right. Kept me stuck there, in the dream. It coming down from the tree, those long black limbs. Stretching out Its hand—that long finger—then turning slowly to look at me— those eyes—always open. Always open. I've got to get something stronger.

6/8/15

Managed to get a prescription for Vicodin. Been on it for the past few days. Flushed the Ambien. Vicodin knocks me out. Keeps things blurry. Sleeping 6-7 hours now. Better. But sometimes I think I've woken up— I'm lying in bed, and everything feels so real—and then I turn, and It's crouched there at the end of the bed—watching me. Those eyes. It stretches out Its arm, like that night in the forest. That one long hooked finger. And the eyes—those big round eyes, looking right into mine. Always open. I can't turn away. So I scream and thrash and wake up—at least I think I wake up—and sometimes It's still there. Still there, looking right at me. So I'm upping the dose.

Millar's next few entries are scattered; no more than a few stray lines, noting the number of hours he slept—which continue to decrease—and the doses of narcotics he takes— which continue to rise. By mid-July, he was taking more than 20 milligrams of Vicodin throughout each day and sleeping less than two hours per night.

That was when Elisa Fournier came to visit. Millar records no details of how she arrived in Kuala Lumpur, or how she found him—he simply states that on July 12, she showed up at his door, ragged from lack of sleep:

6/9/15
. . . *[she has] no idea what happened to Rafaralahy. Hasn't seen him since that night. But she's been having the dreams too. Won't say it in so many words, but I can tell by looking in her eyes. I hate that word. Eyes. She's got to go.*

The next few entries are scattered—but it's clear that Fournier had somehow acquired a bottle of the general anesthetic Propofol, and convinced Millar to try injecting it in surgical doses each night, as she was doing.

As a result of this self-administered treatment, Millar reports an immediate increase in sleeping time, from less than two hours up to a consistent six per night. For nearly a week, he makes no mention of the nightmares. He even alludes to the possibility of returning to his work at the university.

A few days later, however, he makes these entries:

6/11/15
Only two nights' worth of Propofol left. Elisa doesn't know how to get it here—Malaysian drug enforcement is a lot stricter than in Madagascar. I begged her to try, but she says she won't go out on the street "like a damn junkie." We had an argument, and I went to try to get some for myself. But no luck. One of us is going to have to go back to Antananarivo—or to somewhere we can get more Propofol. I can't go back to how it was before. Elisa is no help. Stupid bitch.

6/13/15
Last of the Propofol is gone. So is Elisa. Had a screaming fight, and she ran out. Slammed the door. Won't answer her phone. I'm back on the Vicodin but it's not helping. Can't sleep. Don't want to sleep. I know what I'll see as soon as I close my eyes.

6/16/15
Went to a dodgy neighborhood and tried to score something stronger—anything— heroin, Fentanyl, horse tranquilizer. Nothing. So I'm going the opposite route. Uppers. Got some coke. Amphetamines. Whatever happens, I will not sleep.

6/18/15
Didn't think I fell asleep, but I did. Was there in the forest again. Saw It come down from the tree. Tried to turn away— but everywhere I turned, It was right there. Watching me. Those eyes. More uppers tonight. No more mistakes.

Then, on the following evening, Millar makes an unusually lengthy entry in a firm, neat hand. That entry reads as follows:

This will be my last entry. It's going to come tonight, no matter what I do. I see It every time I close my eyes, and It's still there when I open them. This is hard to explain, but I'm almost not afraid anymore. Whatever It's going to do, it can't be worse than this waiting. So I'm going to put down, as best I can, what happened in the forest that night.

I woke up in the dark, by the campfire, which was down to a flicker. At least, I think I woke up. I wasn't tied down, but I couldn't move. Couldn't even turn my head. Fournier and Rafaralahy were lying nearby, face-up. No sound but the chorus of insects and the distant calls of lemurs.

It came down from a tree. An aye-aye, bigger than any I'd ever seen or heard of—as tall as a man, skeletally thin and covered in black tangled hair. The way It moved was so strange—like a film being played in reverse. Slowly It descended the tree trunk, staring right at me with those huge yellow eyes and their black pinpoint pupils. Always open, gazing straight into me. I couldn't turn away.

It crept across the ground and climbed atop my chest. I felt Its weight, heavy on top of me. Slowly It raised Its arm. Extended Its long middle finger, hooked with a claw. Pointed it right at me. I tried to scream but couldn't even draw a breath. The finger pressed closer, all the while Its eyes looking into mine.

I felt Its finger push in—an alien presence in the soft tissue beside my eye. It wasn't the pain that was worst, but the feeling of being invaded, penetrated, unable to move. It pushed deeper, gently digging, as if for a grub. All the while watching me. Those huge eyes with their pinprick pupils. Unmoving. Staring.

Then, slowly, It withdrew Its finger. Recoiled Its arm. Turned and crept across the clearing to bend over Rafaralahy. That must've been when I blacked out. When I awoke in the morning, people from the village were standing over me, and Fournier and Rafaralahy were gone. A thin trickle of blood run from my eye; encrusted on my cheek.

But I could move again. They led me to the village, and I followed. Everything else, you know from my notes.

I'm going to fall asleep soon. I can feel it. Nothing I can do. When I close my eyes, It will be there. When I open them, It will be there still, looking back at me. Its eyes are always open.

If you find this and translate it, burn it.

20

Of course, I can't burn Millar's journal. The Kuala Lumpur *polis* still have the original, along with digital copies; and they're waiting eagerly for my translation right now. Any facts I distort or hold back will likely be uncovered at some later point in the investigation, which would disqualify me as an inexpert witness, at best. Worse, any attempt to conceal the full details will probably incriminate me as a willful obstructer of justice, and likely get me deported from this country I've come to call my home.

Besides, I'm still not altogether sure how much of Millar's account to believe. Something very strange happened to him in Forest S9; that much is certain. He clearly returned to Kuala Lumpur convinced that he'd suffered something profoundly unnatural, which drove him to acquire the narcotics and stimulants found at the scene of his suicide. The question of what he actually saw, though, continues to gnaw at me.

I decided to perform a bit of unauthorized investigation on my own. I contacted the Université d'Antananarivo's linguistics and their biology departments, pretending to reach out to Professors Rafaralahy and Fournier about their research, acting entirely unaware of their disappearances, and CCing a few of their departmental colleagues "just in case."

From those colleagues, I received the following responses:

From: nfantanera@univ-antananarivo.mg
Date: 29 August, 2015 14:23:56 GMT+3
Subject: Re: Rafaralahy's Paper on Archaic Austronesian Phonemic Structures

Dear Dr. K—

Thank you for reaching out regarding Prof. Rafaralahy's research. It's fortunate you decided to CC me, because Dr. Rafaralahy is currently on indefinite family leave.

Please find attached a PDF of Prof. Rafaralahy's 2008 paper on phonemic structures in isolated austronesian populations.

In answer to your question, Prof. Rafaralahy has expressed an interest in discovering such isolated populations in remote regions of Madagascar. However, this is not a mainstream view in the professional community, and I'm unaware of any scholarly publications—speculative or otherwise—on the existence of such a population on this island.

Kind regards,

Noël Fanantera
Associate Professor of Linguistic Anthropology
Université d'Antananarivo

=======

From: landrianjanaka@univ-antananarivo.mg
Date: 30 August, 2015 09:15:17 GMT+3
Subject: Re: Fournier's Paper on Veneration of Strepsirrhines Among Malagasy Populations

Hello Dr. K—

I'm happy to help as much as I can, given that Prof. Fournier is currently out of the office on family leave.

As you say, Prof. Fournier was particularly interested in tribal groups who, instead of worshipping commonly venerated strepsirrhine species such as the indri and ring-tailed lemur, venerate the aye-aye as dreamking and psychopomp.

Several groups of aye-aye worshippers do indeed live on the east coast of Madagascar—however, I'm unaware of any such groups living in the island's interior. If Prof. Fournier is aware of the existence of such a group, she certainly hasn't published about them.

For reference, I attach a PDF copy of Prof. Fournier's 2005 paper on aye-aye veneration among Sakalava fishermen.

P.S. Your curiosity about Prof. Fournier's work comes as somewhat of a surprise to me. What did you say your specialization was?

Léonie Andrianjanaka
Assistant Chair of Anthropology
Université d'Antananarivo

As Fournier's and Rafaralahy's colleagues make clear, both those professors were convinced of the existence of uncontacted indigenous tribes in the deep jungles of Madagascar—tribes who worshiped the aye-aye—though their colleagues had no suspicion that such tribes actually existed, and neither of the two professors seem to have published any formal research on the topic.

This tight secrecy may have been no more than typical academic politics: in highly competitive departments with limited tenure slots, most researchers clutch their best cards close to their chests until they've collected enough data for a definitive publication. Even so, the fact that these two researchers from separate departments engaged in such a clandestine collaboration—and flew Millar out to perform fieldwork with them—convinces me that they genuinely believed they were on the trail of a career-making discovery.

These, then, are the facts I know for certain: In May 2015, Millar flew to Madagascar to meet with Rafaralahy and Fournier, who convinced him to join them on an expedition to Forest S9. They reached the site where they believed they'd find the uncontacted tribe—whereupon Fournier and Rafaralahy vanished. Millar returned to Antananarivo about a week later, claiming to have no knowledge of his colleagues' whereabouts, or of what had happened to him in the forest. He was subsequently cleared of suspicion and sent back to Kuala Lumpur, where his mental state rapidly deteriorated and his drug use increased, culminating in his self-mutilation and suicide in the early-morning hours of June 20th.

The most obvious conclusion is that Millar murdered his colleagues for reasons unknown, managed to conceal the evidence, and was driven by guilt to commit suicide. But of course, that leaves the question of motive. Did Millar want all the credit for the discovery? He was a highly driven researcher, certainly—but competitive enough to commit a double murder? That doesn't seem to fit the data.

And then, of course, there's the evidence from Millar's journal. Much as I keep trying to discount it as the ranting of an overstressed mind, I just can't get it out of my head. The forest. The night. The thing climbing down from the trees. The eyes. The finger. It's all so specific, so detailed. So consistent from one entry to the next.

Last night was August 20. I stayed up late, poring over Millar's last few entries, looking for anything I might've missed; any turn of phrase I might've mistranslated. I re-read the last few pages of his journal again and again, until every detail was burned into my brain.

At some point, I fell asleep.

  must have been dreaming, because I was there in the jungle at night, unable to move, staring helplessly at the prone forms of Millar and Fournier and Rafaralahy on the ground, motionless next to the dying embers of the fire.

My heart was pounding, so loud I could hear my blood rushing in my ears. But I couldn't move. Couldn't turn my head.

It clambered down from the branches, long-limbed and spindly, covered in tangled black hair. Moving just as Millar had said: like a film unspooling in reverse as it descended the tree trunk, seeming to crawl toward me in slow motion, yet approaching with impossible speed.

Its ears enormous, bat-ears, twitching to sounds beyond the range of hearing; Its snout a wreckage of teeth and pulsing flesh, twitching, scenting me in the dark; Its eyes vast and yellow black pinprick pupils glaring into mine.

It crouched upon my chest, suffocating me, Its head down-turned to face me. Slowly It raised a skeletal arm; a stop-motion limb, trembling as if animated by some unseen puppetry; and It extended its bony middle finger, knot-jointed, tipped in a hooked black claw.

And as those eyes bored into me, black pits in jaundiced seas, that hooked finger pressed into the soft tissue between my eye and the bridge of my nose. It pressed, unrelenting, deeper into the fleshy cavern behind my forehead. I could feel It there; invasive, wrong, penetrating where It should not be.

The finger dug gently behind my eye, probing, insinuating itself deeper into me. All while those unblinking eyes watched me, radiant with malice beyond reckoning.

I don't know how long that finger stayed inside me. At last It withdrew, slowly, and I felt a thin trickle of warm blood running down my cheek. The aye-aye stepped back off my chest, and I gasped a breath. It clambered back to the tree trunk, Its eyes never leaving mine. Always open, watching.

I howled in the way one howls in dreams; my wails no more than thin bleats; weak animal sounds. I bleated and thrashed, or tried to thrash. The forest fell away, and I was in my bed again, gazing up at my apartment's stucco ceiling, the lamp still burning on my desk.

It was still there. It crouched at the end of my bed. Its lips pulled back in a jagged-toothed snarl. It lifted its arm and extended its bony middle finger, pointing straight at me. Its eyes wide and furious, watching me. Always open.

he text above represents the final coherent entry in linguist Daniel K—'s notes on his translation of Prof. Jared Millar's enigmatic journal. Perhaps disappointingly, these notes shed little light on the true reasons for Prof. Millar's suicide—or on Prof. K—'s suicide by hanging on the morning of September 1st, 2015.

One key detail stands out in both cases: before taking their own lives, both Millar and K— attempted, without much success, to excise their own eyes.

MARGARET LETS HER SELF GO
SAMANTHA BRYANT

"She's really let herself go." Margaret heard the two women whisper as she passed them in the grocery store. She wasn't sure who they were, though she had the feeling she'd known them once, before she'd found the Orb.

They meant that she looked unkempt. Teeth, hair, and clothes were petty things, unimportant. In a few more days, she wouldn't need her body anymore. Her work would be complete, and she could leave the awkward sack of flesh behind and live amongst the stars. Soon she really would let her self go. She would never be alone again.

For now, though, she had to keep her body going and that meant giving it energy. She moved quickly through the store, trying to look like she was searching for some particular item until she found an empty aisle. Stopped. She stared at the rows of colorful cans on the shelves before her. It was like the words were written in a language she didn't understand. Or like they had a spell on them that kept her from being able to focus. She pursed her lips and considered. She once knew how to read this language, she was sure. But now, her mind was given over to the people of the Orb, who spoke only in resonances and frequencies. If only the cans could sing their contents to her heart like the Orb did.

She chose a tall, cylindrical container and picked it up. She felt nothing. No vibration in her palm. She studied it again. A picture of a furry creature decorated the label. That didn't seem right. She also didn't see how it opened. She chose another one.

The short, flatter containers had a ring on the top that a person was clearly intended to pull on to get to the contents. The curling script was beautiful. She put a few of those cans into the cart. Moving quickly again, she grabbed a bag from another shelf. It didn't matter to her what these foodstuffs were. Anything would work to keep her body functioning a few more days.

Feeling nervous, she went to the front. Harold had done the shopping ever since her breakdown. It had been years since she'd been inside a store. But she had thought it through step-by-step. She knew what to do. She reassured herself and patted the small bag that hung from her arm. She had brought some of the green paper so valued on this plane. The whole idea of exchanging labor for paper, and paper for goods, just struck her as ridiculous. It would be a relief to end such petty negotiations.

Margaret bounced on her feet, fighting her growing impatience and practicing her lines. It was important to respond appropriately to what the girl said. There was no need to speak aloud when she could just commune with the people of the Orb, mind to mind, soul to soul. Without Harold, she didn't use her voice much. The inside of her mouth was dry and rusty.

"Hello, Mrs. Stevens. Did you find everything you need?" the girl asked.

Margaret forced her head up and down and smiled. "Yes?" she said, hoping that was correct. It must have been, because the girl started moving the cans across the light. The beep startled Margaret. It sounded like the danger warning from the Orb. Surely there could be no danger from the Others here. Reaching into the pocket of her loose pants, she gripped the small dagger again, the handle sliding into her palm with an easy familiarity. She bit the inside of her cheek hard enough that she drew blood. It tasted strong in her mouth, strong and right.

"Did you get a cat?" the girl said.

"A cat?" The word was familiar, but she could attach no meaning to it. Still, she had observed that you could just repeat what you heard, and people would move on. It had worked at the bank when she went to take out the money.

The girl was looking at her strangely. Something was wrong. What had she missed?

She smiled again, forcing the corners of her mouth up and trying to hide the panic that was rising in her like bubbles from the lungs of a drowning man.

It worked. The girl laughed. Margaret echoed the sound, though she had no idea why. Humor had never been easy for her, even before the Orb. Now, it eluded her completely.

"You always were a trip, Mrs. Stevens," the girl said.

"A trip?" Margaret repeated. Was the girl asking about her journey? No one was to know. Secrecy was paramount. If they knew, the Others would stop her. They wanted lower beings kept suppressed. The people of the Orb were heretics in the eyes of the Others because they chose to raise beings from all the planes.

Then the girl announced the amount of green paper that she wanted. Margaret relaxed her grip and let the dagger slide back into the pocket, unused. She passed two pieces of paper to the girl and waited. The girl fed the papers to the machine, held out other papers and some small round pieces of metal Margaret recognized as coins of this land. Margaret took them cautiously and slid them into her bag.

She shuffled forward to where the girl was holding out the bags. The girl touched her arm. Margaret nearly pulled the dagger then, but something held her back. The girl leaned in. "It's good to see you getting out, Mrs. Stevens. Give my best to Mr. Stevens."

Margaret blinked, a big smear of wetness sliding down her cheek. She wiped at it with the back of her hand, trying to understand. Were the girl's words a spell that could pull the liquid from her body? She backed away a step. She couldn't afford the influence of dark magic. She was nearly finished with the purification. They wouldn't take her if she were contaminated. She grabbed the bags and nearly ran from the store.

"Poor woman!" she heard the girl say to someone as she moved towards the doors. "She's never been the same since their daughter died. She'd be lost without Harold. That man is a saint."

Lost? No. Harold had come untethered from this plane. But she had not lost him. She knew where he was. He would be there, waiting for her. Why else would the Orb have begun to glow and sing right as Harold's shell had crumpled to the kitchen floor? It was a sign.

Glowing with the success of her mission, Margaret walked the few blocks to her house. The sun seemed to kiss her skin and she could hear music in the breeze. It echoed the Orb's humming. She increased her pace, anxious to get back to the Circle. As she approached the house, the music grew louder, as if the bones and tissues of her face had picked up the signal and were re-broadcasting the notes in her flesh. She felt her body grow lighter.

Stepping up to the door, Margaret muttered the words that disabled the protection spells she had put in place. Inside, she set the bags on the table. Free from her burdens, she hurried to the central room.

Grateful to have found the Circle intact, Margaret closed her eyes and sent thanks to the People for protecting her work from interference in her absence. She knelt and ran her hands over the sacred objects. They sang their harmonies into her hands. The herbs were still on the silver platter, the candles waiting in the glass bowl. The coins of many lands were organized in the proper pattern around the center ring. All was just as it should be.

Finally, she rested her hand on the Orb. It hummed against her palm, tickling her. Was this what the girl had meant when she asked about a cat? She thought she recalled a similar thrumming coming from a creature with oddly-shaped green eyes, sometime in the Before. She warmed to the vibration now, feeling reassured.

Returning to the bags on the table, she pulled out one of the cans and popped the tab on top. The contents did not please her nose, but she ignored that. Physical senses were not important. They conveyed false and unreliable information. Even while her nose objected to the strange, lumpy looking contents of the can, her stomach rumbled and demanded to receive it. Conflicting signals like this were part of why she wanted to escape the trappings of the flesh and move to a higher plane. Food, bathroom, sleep. Mundane concerns, of no interest. Not when there was the possibility of transcendence.

She stuck her fingers into the soft, mushy meat and sucked it into her mouth. She nearly gagged, but she forced herself to move the nutrients around in her mouth then swallow them. She would not miss having to do this when she was free. A few more swipes and the can was empty. She quickly consumed two more cans, wanting to ensure that her work would go uninterrupted until she could finish. The rumbling in her stomach ceased, replaced by an unpleasant roiling sensation. She ignored it and returned to her work.

She studied her charts and tables. All signs pointed to a window in the next few days, but she still felt uncertain. She needed to make contact.

Returning to the Circle of High Resonance, she lowered herself to the floor. She wrapped the golden ribbon symbolizing her tether to his plane around one wrist. The other end was affixed to the floor itself. She forced herself to calm down before reaching for the Orb. Any other element could be replaced, but the Orb was unique. Without it, all hope was lost.

Wiping her hands on her pants to ensure they were not sweaty or slick, Margaret reached out with two hands, forming a cup with her palms. With her fingertips, she coaxed the Orb until it rolled into the hollow of her cradling hands. Instantly, it began to glow, the bright whiteness casting colorful shadows on the walls through the cracks in her cupped palms. Margaret focused and took a few deep breaths. She concentrated on shutting down her senses.

Vision was both the easiest and the hardest. Simply closing her eyes would stop her from seeing anything, but the mind insisted on creating its own images: Harold's reddened, panicked face; the cold, stiff, painted face they had made for Angie. Suppressing the images was hard, but she was determined. Finally, she achieved a perfect blackness against which she would paint her pathway to the Seventh Plane.

She focused on her hearing next. Even alone in this small shelter, Margaret was accosted by sound. There was a skittering in the walls that she worried might be the Others, trying to break through the protective spells. Even her own body made sounds she could hear in the darkness: a wheezing from the nose, a buzzing in the ears, the pulsing of blood moving through her limbs. She concentrated on the low hum of the Orb until it was all she could hear.

In the silent darkness, Margaret strove to release scent and taste; the twin senses that tethered a person in the lower planes. The food so recently in her mouth made this difficult. Perhaps she should have rinsed her mouth, but if she got up now, she would have to start again. So, she persevered, concentrating hard enough that she began to sweat.

Finally, it was only the sense of touch blinding her. This was the hardest to let go. The other senses shut down, but she was painfully aware of the sensations of the flesh. Her hips complained about the position she maintained. Her skin seemed to crawl, whether from warmth or some other cause, she didn't know.

She focused intently on the black empty space she had created in her mind, trying to vanquish all awareness of the physical. Her head fell back, and she pulled the Orb to her heart. Her pulse slowed and came into sync with the Orb's, just as it had the first time the people had contacted her.

She reached out, calling gently with her heart's song—Harold? Ha-rold? She persevered, even when she was met with no response. She called his name until the words became a chant without meaning, a string of nonsense syllables—haroldharoldharoldharoldharold.

Finally, she felt it, a vibration. She didn't open her eyes to look, afraid to break the spell, but she knew that if she had, the Orb would now be glowing and floating, its soft light filling the shelter. When she finally opened her eyes, she could no longer see the room she knew her body still rested in. Instead she was at the center of a sea of light. She recognized the colorful swirls as the people. She wanted to look down at herself, but "down" was not a concept that made sense in this space, nor was "self." A light blue swirl of color spun into a corkscrew shape, which Margaret understood as a greeting. She wondered how the people saw her. Did she look like a swirl of color or was "look like" another construct that didn't apply? Maybe the swirls of color were only there to accommodate her, in her limited perceptions.

The time for idle curiosity was long past. Time was mostly meaningless for the People, but they seemed to understand her urgency. Pushing past words to pure thought, Margaret struggled to open her mind to the probes of the people. There was pain deep in her head, seated in the brain.

Despite her wish to cooperate, something in her physiology resisted the invasion. She'd always heard that the brain did not have nerve endings. Psychological or not, the pain was quite real. She gritted her teeth and endured. She wasn't going to let pain stop her.

When the probing ceased, Margaret almost collapsed with relief. But she knew there was more to come. She braced herself for the flurry of images. All communication from the people had been like this: fast, direct, and incomprehensible at first. This time was no different.

Her mind was awash in a green glow, and through it she could see Harold smiling at her. He was holding hands with Angie. Angie, all smooth and bright again, not mangled and broken. Neither of them spoke, but seeing her, they turned and held out their arms to her. She could almost feel the warmth of their embrace.

"When?" A vision appeared. The kitchen calendar. She saw the red markings on the calendar. Tomorrow, on the confluence of threes. The anniversary. Margaret nodded. It had a nice synchronicity.

The directions came in flashed images. Then she could see Harold and Angie again, their smiles glowing white as they faded into the starlight.

Wilting, Margaret dropped her head to her chest, the connection fading. She wiped her wet face on her sleeves. Angie had been perfect, beautiful as she had been before the car had crumpled around her, and Harold's face was open in a way she hadn't seen in years. No worry clouding the corners of his eyes. No sadness pulling his shoulders down.

Tomorrow. Only a few hours! She was so excited and, at the same time, so scared. Her joy was intermixed with other, complicated emotions. Margaret took a deep breath. There was no time for doubt now. Harold could only stay in the interstitial plane a short while.

Margaret stood, wobbling unsteadily. She had hated this body for so long. It ached when the weather was cold. The heaviness of it, like a prison her lighter soul was unaccountably bound to. Yet now, thinking of letting it go, she found she had some affection for the thing after all. She would miss the smell of spring, the texture of a soft blanket against her skin. It had served her well, this fleshy holding cell.

Looking down, Margaret noticed the stain in the center of her shirt. She remembered that she had a fondness for this particular garment. Harold said she looked beautiful in it. The blue jewel-tone complimented her eyes.

Absently, she turned and entered the bathroom. She turned on the shower, waiting until it filled the room with steam. She dropped the stained shirt into the overflowing hamper, grimacing at the feel of her matted, greasy hair against her fingers.

Margaret stepped into the shower, the steam overwhelming with the sensations of drops bouncing against her flesh. Once she had enjoyed long showers. Harold would come knocking and ask if she was ever coming out. She'd say she couldn't, there was still hot water left. Raising her face into the stream now, Margaret wished Harold would come and scrub her back.

Stepping out, she pulled a towel from the shelf and wrapped herself in it. She felt wonderful. Cleanliness was part of the purification. She ran over the details of the vision again, making a list of items she would need.

But first, she wanted to check on Harold. It wasn't Harold anymore. She knew that. But it still brought her comfort to be near the shell that had once held him. Still wrapped in her towel, she went to the room that had been Angie's.

As Margaret entered, pain gripped her mind and blinded her for a moment. She leaned against the doorframe waiting for her vision to clear, pushing down the dark images that accosted her. The Others were trying to bind her to this plane with pain and loss, but she would not give in. Harold and

32

Angie were waiting. They would all be one with the stars.

Harold's shell was on its back. She had dragged it there from the kitchen and pulled it onto the bed. Now, she sat on the edge of the bed and rested a hand on one of his hands. A liquid feeling rushed up her arm, washing over her like a wave in a sun-warmed lagoon. She let her gaze travel up the body to the face. It was still frozen in an expression of surprise and joy, mouth agape and eyes wide. She smiled down at him, and stroked his face, smoothing down his hair.

Returning to their bedroom, she opened the closet and looked for something to put on. Clothes seemed a silly thing to be concerned about in the face of eternity, but her flesh was growing cold in the towel. She wouldn't be able to concentrate if she were shivering. Maybe the body knew its time was short and wanted its comforts for the end.

Now dressed, Margaret lingered in the closet, until she was startled by a pounding sound. The sound came again, and Margaret gradually came to realize that it was someone knocking on the door.

She moved to the window and peeked out at the porch at a woman she didn't know. At least she didn't think she did. Seeing that she was raising her hand to knock again, Margaret opened the door a crack and peered out. "Margaret?" the woman said.

"Yes?" she responded cautiously.

"I just wanted to make sure you're all right. There were strange lights coming through your windows."

"I'm fine," she said. The woman peered into the opening, trying to see around Margaret into the living room and beyond. Margaret stood so that she blocked the view.

"You sure? I haven't seen Harold in a day or two. Is he sick?"

"On a trip," she said. She quickly closed the door and hurried back to the Circle. The time was now. Clearly, the Others had sent the woman. She peered out the curtains beside the door and saw the meddlesome busybody already on her phone.

Moving with a sureness she seldom felt anymore, Margaret removed her clothing and lay down, resting the Orb on her abdomen. With an overwhelming rush of relief that the waiting was finally over, she let herself go blank.

A blue flashing light reflected in the glass of the windows and bounced around the room. The door burst open and a large shape in a long coat filled the doorway. It was one of the Others, but he was too late to stop her.

Closing her eyes, she lifted the Orb in her cupped hands toward the sky. The ceiling slid

33

away, and she could see the whirling cosmos above. The Orb began to spin in her hands, then lifted away, filling the room with its pure, white glow. Her body lifted into the air and took on the same bright glow. Far below, she heard the dark-coated Other call out, "What the hell?"

A radio crackled and a woman cried out. "Get her down! This can't be happening!"

Margaret spared little thought for the people witnessing her departure. She felt her atoms spread out into the darkness, streaking upward and upward, until they intermingled with the People. All feeling of Margaret dissipated like so much smoke. She was one with the people. The Others couldn't reach her now. She had let her self go.

SPLIT THROUGH THE SKY
LENA NG

 n evil has tainted my sleep. More than night terrors, what skin-crawling, de-filed, and heaving abomina-tions have come to plague me in my dreams. Body twitching and seizing until, in the dead of night, my eyes flung open, overstretched, to stare des-pairingly through my bedroom window into the endless, dark night canvas. Instead of stars, the pinpricks of light seemed as holes where an unknown, unfathomable voyeur was spy-ing from the other side of the nocturnal sky as through a camera obscura.

The second night, horrors most urgent bled from my ears. The insectoids scurried beneath the thread-bare blan-kets and scuttled over my skin.

Nightmares made phantasmagoria crawled through my orbits to tattoo scarification patterns on the insides of my eyelids. The patterns mimicked the unsettling pattern of the stars.

The third night, a humanoid people in blasphemous tongues muttered in my sleep. They pointed at me and drew a star pattern in the dirt. Beyond their goatish eyes and snouts, some strange familiarity in their facial features, primordial ancestors in my reincarnated past danced and gestured an obscene beckoning to join them.

Before I had gone to bed on the first night of torments, I had noticed a disturbing alignment of stars. Through mathematics, the stars and planets should follow a predictable elliptical path. But the planets of Versiveus, Kraelov, and Diaxon, moved in enigmatic, unnerving voyages. Other stars crossed in horrendous formations, and I quaked at what such signs could mean. Whereas seers, prophets, and oracles read portents in tea leaves, in the scattering of bones, in the twist of lines on palms, I could read warnings in the positioning of outer planets, the fleeing of corrupted stars, and the burning of Azurrabed's comet, their bizarre and unpredictable movements in the black canvas of the cosmos not foreseeable by any astronomer or scientist.

Nor had my dreams contained the usual symbols and images of falling, fleeing, or flying. The fragmented glimpses of mesentery-moist, pulsing, flesh-like megacilia could mean a multitude of ambiguities and insinuations and I fled to the underground libraries for answers. The cowled, tongue-less monks accepted my bodypound and I smelled the burning of my sacrifice as I followed the silent shroud of the monk deeper into the labyrinth of tunnels. He performed the crucial signs, sang the voiceless canticle, and the vault doors to the Deep Room, notched with protective rites, clanked open.

Frantically, feverishly, I delved into the delirium-inducing *Mortemordis*, poured through the curse-riddled *Gorgonology* using antidote-laced gloves, and studied the abhorrent *Maledictory*. Even locking myself in a fetid room with the *Almanac Enigmata*, the poison book of knowledge, could not answer my questions. I left when I began to weep blood.

Back in my studio, page after page I flung to the floor as I drew diagrams, scribbled equations, created derivatives and reductions of the movements of the stars, knowing the patterns of the celestial formation must be part of a grander design. Not the math of this world but the math of the parallel: non-Newtonian geometry, Fortunado's topology, octrine trigonometry. Not even the black calculus of Crucerbus could decipher the malevolent pattern.

After a week of haunted nights, tired and with a suffocating blanket of dense depression which ground my bones, I paid a visit to my great uncle, my only living relative though I had not spoken a word to him since I had finished my studies. Both my parents had died when I was a child and my secluded great uncle funded my upbringing and education. He was a grey, morbid man, his skin a pool of wrinkles, his frame seemingly stirred by a thread of will which animated his body like a puppet. I told him of the primeval people who beckoned me to join them, the foreboding alignment of the stars, the flash of animal-human hybrids that mutilated their fleshy forms in profane ways. When I spoke of these horrors, his face blanched as though he had seen the unnamed visions, the impure inferno, the contaminated images conjured before him.

He knew this day would come; he had told me. He had read the signs. He had heard it in the crow's screech, saw it in the psoriatic cirrocumulus clouds, and he trembled beneath the ominous stratocumulus sky.

He arose from his sunken chair, and from a gold chain around his neck, he pulled forth a twisted key like that of a skeletal finger. This key was used to unlock a base metal box, carved patterns on its sides like a demonic, hellish puzzle box. From his box he took out a yellowed ugly leathery papyrus that I came to realize was made from human skin.

"Here," he said as he thrust those papers into my hands, "your real name."

As I opened the dried, wrinkled skin paper, the unclean hieroglyphics undulated on the page, no letters in any human language decipherable. With this unpronounceable name came papers outlining my adoption at birth. This explained the remoteness of the parents I had known, Fabien and Magdalene Vigilius, so distant growing up, so lacking in warmth and parental affection. They were instead my gatekeepers, my guardians, my family of strangers. I played alone, ate alone as my parents watched as distant silent observers. However, my true ancestors, the ancestors of my dreams, called to me.

Upon retrieving the documents, my great uncle sank back into his chair. He said, "You were adopted through the Gentrocide agency, in Blackheart, New England. They may have more revelations for you." After he uttered these words, it was as though his purpose had been completed and he collapsed, shrunken into a desiccated corpse before mine eyes.

lackheart, New England. From my research, a barren hamlet with abandoned decrepit buildings set like battered teeth on salted, charred earth. Once a rural village in the late seventeenth century surrounded by crops of squash, beans, and corn before a Puritan offshoot religion grew more extremist. Medieval extraction techniques such as foot roasting, hamstringing, and de-nailing led to confessions of the practice of blood sorcery. The accused were hanged, burned, and drowned.

So much innocent blood was spilled on the land that it ruined the earth, and guilt and insanity drove out the remaining settlers. Over the years, new colonists looking to return to the old ways in a fundamentalist folly, would try to settle the land for another rebirth of the village. But the befouled land could not sustain the population and the settlement would eventually die again. It was during one of these resettlements that the Gentrocide Orphanage came into existence.

Before undertaking a trip to this sinister locale, I decided to investigate other methods to delve into my twisted, enigmatic roots. I swabbed my cheek to give samples to

genealogy decoders, to find if I could unravel my family tree through the secrets within the coding of my cells. They mapped out my genes. Long strands of deoxyribonucleic acid formed helical patterns of adenine, thymine, guanine, and cytosine. But shockingly, other nitrogen bases, non-human ones, were also identified: dendrosine, and parnadrine, lytonine, and monomotomine.

The scientific methods could not determine my heritage. Long segments were marked inconclusive, or nonhuman but no explanation could be ascertained. 29% unknown ancestry. No relatives traced on the cyber genealogy tree.

If I am not fully human, then what am I? Resurrected through recombinant gene-splicing? Hybridal chimera, part-human, part-nightmare?

y plane, by train, and by foot, I made my journey, my driver quick to surrender me alone to the thick forest when he read a road sign citing "The Path of Righteousness." By compass and coordinates I would find my way to Blackheart. The shivering woods were gloomy, dark and deep, and the crows screeched themselves hoarse against me in the descending light. The scuffle of my feet on dead leaves sounded as though I were a monster stalking the woods.

My knapsack weighed heavier on my shoulders the longer I trudged through the woods. Despite the thickness of the forest canopy, without urban light, I saw clearer the unexplained calibration of the stars and felt naked beneath them.

It was close to dawn when I reached the outskirts of an outcropping of a dozen buildings, the decaying village of Blackheart. Nature had reclaimed the land. Vines of ivy tangled an insidious stranglehold over the crumbling stone buildings. The make-shift roads were empty and long weeds pushed through the crumbling paving. The silence was empty, and it seemed to be everywhere.

A copper-green plaque by the door alerted me to the Gentrocide Orphanage. The orphanage looked as though built as an old brick church, a morose, lachrymosal building. Four windows with faded black shutters stood guard on either side of a black-painted door. The door creaked as I opened it. The interior of the building seemed colder than the exterior, a psychic as well as physical cold, and breath transformed into apparitions. Charcoal shadows seemed burnt into the walls, as though an atomic bomb had detonated and blasted the shadows from the occupants. When I listened closely, I could hear a faint scratching emanating from behind the aging plaster. Likely rats or other vermin, and I had no desire to discover its inhabitants.

In a logical manner, I would start from the second storey of the building and work my way downward. Vile moisture ran down the walls like a sickly sweat. The breathy sounds of scurrying centipedes under watchful spider eyes. Glowing disembodied stares seemed to follow my every move as I wound my way up the rickety staircase to the upper level.

The door to the first room already stood open. It was a large rectangular room with three rows of empty cribs. The walls were painted a cloying green, peeling in some spots, large lace-like splashes of mould on others. The suffering of the prior inhabitants infused the walls, the atmosphere. My imagination, or at least I hoped it was only the imagination, heard the ghostly crying of children.

The next room held hole-ridden, rotting furniture where termites and wood-borers feasted. A writing desk, a splintered chair, and five filing cabinets set against the mould-splashed walls that sent up clouds of rancid dust as I went through their contents. The wood broke as I yanked the locked desk drawer open. A box, which I dashed upon the floor, contained yellowed leathery papers with slash-marked hieroglyphics.

When I touched these papers, the house began to creak. A loud wailing sound swept through the house and the floor beneath my feet began to shudder. The walls bulged rhythmically, as though a giant wormy heart had awoken within the plaster.

I fled the building as though a pack of demons pursued me.

 felt as I had brought home a curse. The slash marks danced on its yellowed skin, and no matter where I was in my house, I felt its malignant presence. At night, it whispered venomous secrets that crept on the edge of consciousness. The mutterings infected my dreams. In my night's visions, the stars grew brighter, larger, and seemed to sprout teeth.

I sought audience with the highest professors of the Occult University, linguistic savants of the opaque, unspeakable languages. The University, a brutalist monolith, was hewn from stone and ornamented with petrified blackwood. The rooms were star-shaped, and through the bending of the other dimensions, there were an infinite number of them. The mosaic flooring resembled the waves of the ocean, burgeoned with unnamed creatures, and the ceiling was patterned with stars.

The twelve monks grew silent as I brought forth the yellowed page. They burned cleansing herbs and chanted obsessively in an infrasonic language before touching the document but even then, there were no guarantees of protection.

Finally, after much consultation through incantations and incense, oratory and arguments, they referred me to High Priestess Narinka, a cleric who lived in the ruins of an Oracular temple in southern Notambishi. She had foreseen the death of the New Redeemer, the outbreak of the white pestilence, and the first wave of the Third Coming, the horrors from which had struck her blind. But her sight with the third eye, the eye which sensed the reality beyond, grew exponentially more powerful, a sense that had grown more acute from the loss of another. She had no age; she was as old as time. She suffered no fools, however. Many fortune hunters, if they had not perished in the journey, had been driven mad in her presence. Four monks, having reached the upper echelons of euphorical meditation, and armed with binding amulets, agreed to take me to the site.

Seven days we spent climbing up mountainside where the air was thin and altitude sickness had us bent and gasping. Seven days bitten by insects the size of our palms, leaving eye-sized welts. One monk developed a sweating sickness and died after convulsing. Another disappeared one night, deep in the middle of Mandire's Forest, presumably abandoning the journey.

At last we reached the stone steps at the mountain's peak leading to her temple. I joined hands with the remaining monks and repeated their incantations before we took the first step. They continued their chanting until we reached the top of the stairs, blanketed by fog. The red columns of the temple were engraved with prayers.

The High Priestess's face was round and smooth, with a cupid-bow mouth, mask-like in its serene perfection, with a cluster of eight eyes that took up much of her forehead.

The two remaining monks' droning chant rose in volume. I took out the yellowed document from my bag, sank to my knees, and pushed the paper towards her. The eight eyes glowed with a pearly sheen. She brushed the tip of her foreleg against the leathery paper. She split her mouth open and lightly tapped me with her mandibles which had extruded from within. I tried not to tremble under her arachnid caress. A thin, curved fang pushed out and pierced me through my cheek. She tasted the drop of blood using a long pink tongue.

"Yesss," she hissed, "so now is the time." The eight eyes turned upward to the sky. "You are the catalyst, the key to the door. Go to the place of your birth. Follow the River Aox until you find its source."

She watched me as I stood. I backed away from her until I reached the start of the stairs before I fled. The blood had whetted her appetite and she took one monk as an offering.

The place of my birth. The River Aox, a holy river where local people believed that bathing in its waters would free them from the cycle of life and death, grew narrow and more winding as the last monk and I followed it upstream. The thick forest gave way to long grasses and tangled, rope-like vines the width of my wrist. Finally, we were met with an abattoirial circular stone inscribed with hieroglyphics.

As the monk stepped onto this formation, the atmosphere grew oppressive and bristled with warning. A slicing sound cut through the air. The monstrous vegetation, with its tendrils, lashed around the final monk until he looked spooled as a ball of twine. The living jungle pulled him by the limbs into the sky.

In a whiplash, the vines retracted, the speed of which cut into his skin. He fell onto the stone and bled to death before me, a death by thousands of cuts, the stone absorbing the blood.

I ran but there was no need to pursue me. The tendrils snapped around and dragged me to the circular stone. From there the vines retracted and from the lashes flowed my blood. Instead of crimson, the fluid glowed with an ominous phosphorescence. At its taste, the stone beneath me splintered, the sound thundering in my ears.

Above, the dark sky cracked open, and from this eggshell split, an unnatural infernal octrine light, a vomitus yellow-green from the deep outer infinity of the cosmos, shone through. Masses of squirming, pink-fleshed appendages, glistening moist from the universe's mucosal lining, thrashed their way twisting through the split, like an eruption of monstrous worms in a radiation pit. Cup-shaped mouthparts rhythmically suctioned open and shut while hordes of giant tick-like parasites scuttled over the organ-raw mass.

My eyes couldn't encompass the horrific imageries. The vitreous liquid contained within my eyes boiled, and from the toxicity of the visions, the eyeballs burst within the sockets, scorching the scarification tattoos beneath my eyelids. I should have been blind, but the octrine-vile light opened my third eye, the eye which allows us to see into the multiplicity of dimensions and I was cursed with a hideous knowledge.

The translated letter described how I was meant for slaughter. The code lay in my cells, my blood, the key pattern to opening this hell-world with the proper alignment of the stars. I was born to be sacrificed to the Ancient Ones under a bleeding moon in the centre of pentagonating stars but was snatched away by the remnants of a fundamentalist missionary sect.

Now with the stars above once again in formation, the spilling of my blood the key, I saw the gibbering slave-priests, my dream-kin who had called to me in the unconscious nether realm, grovelling in eternal madness to the gods Goreth, Ramsire, and Baphthmotet. Commonly known as The Triumvalent, the Unhallowed Trinity, from whom our human concoction of Satan or the devil is but a weak facsimile, the true entities infinitely more evil, infinitely more conflicting, delighting in destruction and in everything which is in opposition to the good and righteous. Its spirit is encompassing, infecting all parts of human nature, so we ground down those already fallen into the dust. My blood ushered in the new world as I was tormented in hideous helplessness upon a fractured altar.

Above, an acidic sticky toxin rained down and burned raw holes in my body. The smell of sizzling flesh contaminated the air. Outpoured forth from the widening split in the sky hailed vast monstrous creatures—deities—from the nether-dimensional realms. The flaming, long-toothed Snakehead . . . the chimeral, dual-tongued Lizardwalker . . . The hoofed, unbounded Goatman with the split, weeping eyes. . . .

SERINCIA, *OR*:
THE AMOURS OF DEATH
SCOTT J. COUTURIER

Ihe maid Serincia was of such beguiling cast
that all came seeking her blushing hand.
Peasants, poets, kings, men-before-the-mast
& stranger suitors from antique, sun-blasted lands
all competed for her fiercely unfelt love.
Yet, she was cool & placid as a rill subterrene,
so remote that it Death himself behove
to revere her beauty, & crave her as his Queen.

A terrible thing, to feel keenly the lust of Death!
Reeking from the endlessly replenished grave
he bore her bouquets of lavender & withered baby's breath,
& his sepulchral troth freely, effusively gave.
Terrified as only mortal youth can be
by Death's unceasing, arduous supplications
Serincia decided secretly that she would flee
the house of her father, forsaking her duty & her station.

For surely Death was drawn by the thousand eyes
that beheld her, the wine-stained lips that spewed her praise?
Thus, under a beggar-woman's uncomely guise
she embarked one nightfall to the rotting quays.
Far she traveled, caked in deliberately teeming filth,
her beauty quick-belabored, spent on worldly grief;
yet her misery merely yielded fertile tilth
for Death's desire to attain her love's relief.

Across the wind-scoured mountains of Soor-mi-Lang
& the mephitic, ruin-studded swamps of Modex,
to the antipodal strands of brine-damp sands
on archipelagos nameless in chart or codex,
Serincia fled always Death's o'er-amorous shade –
yet always he came, bearing severed heads
or orchids plucked from some charnel glade
where battle had sewn the dirt thick with dead.

Finally, warped and haggish with lifelong dread
Serincia found her headlong flight sore impeded
by the ceaseless exhaustion each motion bred
& the pain each plodding step mercilessly out-meted.
Weathered, weary, sick to bones cold-fraught,
she at last staggered into Winter's enwombing blast,
inviting Death to steal what Life had fiendishly bought:
thus, the amours of oblivion won her love at last.

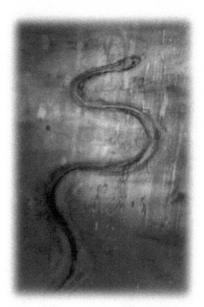

CALL ME BY MY NAME
MARGE SIMON & ALESSANDRO MANZETTI

esterday I was a King,
an astronaut of love,
and like a drunken surrealist,
I painted my body in red and purple,
with spidery green goddesses.

Down along my thin legs,
I drew a South American landscape,
only a few square meters of rainforest
entwined with the Amazon's capillaries.
I was down there, I became the river
—call me Mar Dulce—
chasing the water dragon,
with its slimy and slippery skin,
of an unchangeable joy.
But I did it, I grabbed that whipping tail,
and it coiled around my dry wrists

eagerly looking for the juice of day.

I dreamed I was a Peruvian monkey
being levitated long enough
to taste my banana
before a lab assistant turned the switch,
slamming me to the floor
—Call me by my name, whatever it may be—
I saw Kahlo's ghost at my window.
and dreamed she embraced me,
consuming all my colours
sucking my tropical tattoos
into her dark pelvis.

Like the ocean, my sorrow
became borderless.
Kiss me, what is taking so long?
—Call it *black salt*, it's kind of like the perfect storm—
Swallow my seconds, drink me
like a boiling mojito, show me how much
you like to see me die, each time,
sucked by a deep dark hole,
a perfect zeo drawn
on the canvas of my own skin.

HOW TO SET WRITING GOALS YOU ARE SURE TO ACHIEVE
MELISSA BURKLEY

here are generally two times of the year that writers set goals: New Year's and NaNoWriMo. But if you really want to be successful, you should be constantly setting new writing goals for yourself.

But when it comes to writing goals, not all are created equal. Certain goals are more likely to be achieved than others. Surely, we've all had the experience of setting a writing goal (or even a non-writing goal) and failing to achieve it. So how can you make sure that the writing goals you set for yourself are ones that will ensure success?

The good news is that psychological scientists have done the hard work for you. Decades of research has uncovered a few simple secrets that if you follow, will guarantee that the goals you set are ones you'll actually achieve.

Essentially, it all comes down to this: Smart people set S.M.A.R.T. goals.

Specific

irst, your writing goal should be *specific*. A major reason people fail at their goals is that they define them too vaguely. For example, saying, "I want to write a novel" is much vaguer than saying "I want to write a chapter for my novel every month." And saying, "I want to get my shorts stories published" is vaguer than saying, "I want to write five short stories and submit them by the end of the summer." Making your writing goal-specific gives you greater clarity on exactly what you want and how to get it. Plus, specific goals are less overwhelming because they take a big, looming task like writing a novel or getting published and break it into small, more manageable parts.

Measurable

econd, your writing goal should be *measurable*. This just means defining your goal in numerical terms. By doing this, you get two birds with one stone because not only does it make your goal measurable, it automatically makes it specific too!

You have several options when it comes to making your goal measurable. For example, you could define your goal in terms of number of pages, chapters or short stories ("I want to submit five of my short stories to top magazines"). Or instead, you could do what I do and define your goal by word count ("I want to write 1000 words a day for my novel").

By quantifying your goal in this way, it becomes far easier to tell if you are succeeding at your goal or failing. Notice how hard it is to tell if you are currently failing at the goal to "write a novel," but it is plainly obvious when you are failing at the goal to "write a chapter a week." Quantifying your goal in this way helps you identify early on if you are falling short of your goal and then you can adjust your behavior accordingly. Plus, it gives you an accurate sense of how much effort and time is required to succeed at your goal.

Accountable

hird, your writing goal should be *accountable*. It is one thing to set a goal for yourself; it is another to tell others about your goal. The stakes for failure aren't very high when we are the only ones to know about our writing goal. But when we tell others about our goal and we fail, we often experience a windfall of shame and guilt. Tons of studies show that if you make your goal public in some form—this could be telling

your loved ones, the members of your writer's group, finding a writing buddy in your online community, or posting your goal on social media—you are more likely in the end to actually achieve your goal. So, whatever your writing goal is, don't keep it a secret.

Realistic

ourth, your writing goal should be *realistic*. Or to state it another way, your goal should be reasonably attainable given your level of experience and your talents. We all wish we could magically write 10,000 words a day (and there a few crazy writers out there who claim they can) but such a goal is completely unrealistic, especially if you have a full-time job, a family that actually wants to see you face-to-face, or any other number of obligations.

Overly enthusiastic writers (aka writing novices) often make this fatal mistake or starting out with unattainable goals. They leap out of the starting gate with an unrealistic idea of what they want to accomplish and as a result, practically guarantee that they will fall flat on their face.

So, what is a realistic writing goal? It depends on who you ask.

Hemingway supposedly wrote 500-1000 words a day. Instead, Stephen King writes about 2000 words a day, every single day (even on his birthday and Christmas). But King recognizes that not everyone has the luxury to be a full-time writer like himself, so in his excellent book *On Writing* he suggests you aim for 1,000 words a day. Or if you are a fan of Julia Cameron's suggestion to do morning pages (based on her advice book *The Artist's Way*), you can hit 750 words at the start of each day. The point is this: it is easy to identify an unrealistic goal, but only you can determine what an attainable goal is for you personally.

My advice: if you are a writer struggling to find time to write, start with a goal of 500 words a day (or if you prefer time, 30 minutes a day). Once you consistently hit that goal, ratchet it up to 750 or 1,000 words. And if you struggle to even hit 500 words, lower the bar a bit and strive for 200 words. It may take you longer to finish your novel but even with a small goal like that, you will eventually finish if you stick with it. Sometimes slow and steady is the only way you can finish the race, and that's okay, so long as you actually finish.

Time-Bound

astly, your writing goal should be *time-bound*. This means you should assign deadlines to your writing goal. You can (and should) do this in two ways. First, assign an overarching end-date to your overall goal. For example, if you want to write a novel, give yourself a reasonable deadline for when you want to have the first draft finished. Second, and perhaps more importantly, break up your goal into mini-goals and assign these deadlines along the way. So instead of saying, "I will work on my novel this week" you could say, "I will write for an hour a day five days this week." Or instead of saying, "I want to submit my short stories this year" you could say, "Every Friday I will spend one hour on Duotrope identifying desirable markets for my stories and then submitting them."

Summary

kay, so let's put it all together now. If your goal is to write a novel this year, try setting a goal like this: "I will write 1,000 words a day (specific/measurable/realistic) five days of the week (time-bound). I will tell my best friend about my goal and tell them to check in weekly and make sure I am sticking to it (accountable)." See how much harder it is to slack on this goal compared to the standard "I will write a novel this year"?

Before I leave you, here is one additional piece of advice: To make it even more likely that you will achieve your writing goal, take a moment to actually write down your goal on a Post-It or notecard and stick it in a location that you will see every day. For example, I write my goals on Post-Its and stick them on the bathroom mirror or on the corner of my TV, but you could also put them on the fridge, your laptop, or wherever they will serve as a constant reminder of what you want to achieve.

CARNIVOROUS LUNAR ACTIVITIES
BY MAX BOOTH III
A GEHENNA POST REVIEW

arnivorous Lunar Activities follows two characters: Ted, a man who has just sabotaged his own marriage, and Justin, his childhood friend who calls Ted and soon reveals a shocking and disturbing truth concerning his own recent nocturnal experiences. The novel rapidly picks up pace, and before the reader realizes it, they're knee-deep in a blood-soaked, popcorn page-turner that is likely going to breathe new life into the Werewolf genre.

What really separates Booth's novel from others is the fact that this story is sentient, almost self-aware in its nature. It never takes itself too seriously, and in a meta-fashion, expresses the readers' own absurd thoughts concerning Justin's long bouts of dialogue where he explains the insane, wild ride that led to his current predicament. There are bizarre moments that add to the absurdity, such as Justin tying himself to an anchor as he anticipates his transformation, and also gut-wrenchingly emotional scenarios where Ted comes to terms with his own sins and the people he's affected along the way.

Neither character is clean–both literally and figuratively–and this is something that really adds to the atmosphere of the novel. Ted and Justin are as close as a writer can get to portraying realistic, flawed characters, even if they're not the most savory of individuals. Their experiences and childhood memories feel genuine, and there's not a moment during their conversations that feels forced or unnatural. Booth's decision to lock down the first half of the book with dialogue and an enclosed space was genius, and it builds claustrophobia for the readers, which is a theme that can be felt throughout the novel's narrative. When the story finally does leave Justin's basement, it detonates.

We have to emphasize how powerful Booth's voice is throughout the novel. Every sentence bursts from the page, and both Ted and Justin have such strong personalities, it's as if they're in the room with us, and we're passerby who have become too curious to look away and stop listening. Booth's consistent referencing of *An American Werewolf in London* isn't by accident, as the inspiration is evident with our narrative and the dark humor laced throughout. There are plenty of hilarious moments that Booth masterfully sprinkles in amidst the grotesque descriptions and filthy atmosphere that seeps with every line of dialogue. This novel is meant to gross out the reader, and despite that, Booth never overreaches with the nastiness.

Black Comedy is a difficult subgenre to write in, but Booth shows no restraint in his conquering of it with his crisp language and ability to understand exactly the type of novel he's writing. The author's voice is one of the strongest we've ever read, and though *Carnivorous Lunar Activities* is definitely a quick read, it is nonetheless unforgettable in its quality and focused direction. Werewolves have never been this funny, and the gory nature of their origins and transformations have never been scarier. There's a certain human element to Justin's crises, and it's not what you'd expect. Whereas most Werewolf stories are designed to make you feel sympathy for the kindhearted, wholesome characters, we don't get that here. Yeah, we feel bad that Justin's going through this, but not due to his kind nature. Rather, it's because he is as flawed as a real person, even if his moral compass is a bit more questionable than most. We see someone who has good memories and has experienced joy, but who is also often detestable and who's made a lot of mistakes. This is perhaps where Booth's voice is strongest, in the fact that he can depict a character that we shake our head at but also ravenously enjoy reading.

The relationship between Justin and Ted is definitely the star of the novel, and we see true, undying friendship between them. Their witty banter and crude remarks are enough to make any reader laugh out loud, all at the same time tickling that warm place in our hearts reserved for our own best friends and fondest memories. This theme is seen from the first call Justin makes to Ted, and all the way to the final lines. They're the kind of friends that pick up right where they left off after not seeing each other for years. The type that would do just about anything for each other, while also enjoying the art of antagonizing one another. Booth's novel is a showcase for character dynamics that many writers will likely use as a template for their own work in the future, and the author's mastery of dialogue and fast-paced storytelling will undoubtedly claim a new wave of fans for the writer.

Werewolf stories are an old dog, but Max Booth III has taught the genre some new tricks. We encourage each and

53

every one of you to order *Carnivorous Lunar Activities*, as it is easily in the bracket for best horror novel of 2019 thus far, and we are excited to hear your thoughts when you experience this highlight of personal horror.

SEFIRA & OTHER BETRAYALS
BY JOHN LANGAN
A LISA QUIGLEY
GEHENNA POST REVIEW

early daily, I am blown away by the quality, diversity, and profusion of talent that is available for the consumption of horror readers. The work of John Langan is no exception, and his latest collection *Sefira and Other Betrayals* deserves to be promoted to the top of your TBR pile yesterday—but since it is only just available, today will have to suffice.

The title story "Sefira"—a novella that could easily carry its own weight as a standalone piece and would alone make this entire book worth the purchase—opens this collection with the words, "Lisa looked in the rearview mirror and saw that her eyes had turned black." And just like that, I'm swept away, mesmerized by not only my own needs for answers, but by the clarity of the worlds Langan creates and breathes life into. No two stories are quite the same, and yet they are linked—not only by the common theme of "betrayal," but also by the strength and surety of Langan's writing.

There is nothing like the feeling of giving yourself over completely to an author who knows exactly where he is taking you. You yourself are not always quite sure where you are, though you know it looks familiar; it's this familiarity that drives your need to know more, to finally understand. You're in a world that is something like this one, but slightly different, and yet, you know you've been here before. Maybe you've seen hints of this place in a dream or almost—but not quite—hidden in the dark corners of your bedroom in the middle of the night. The juxtaposition of your understanding that although you're in some place that is utterly new, you've also, somehow, been here before sends you hurtling forward through the narrative. You're terrified to keep going, yet unable to turn back—you must know what it is this author wants to show you, yet you have the sneaking suspicion that *you've known all along*.

This is what it feels like to read each of these stories. Langan compels you forward with the sheer force and surety of his voice, promising, if not exactly comfort, at the very least, commiseration. Here is an author who understands, more than anything, the plight of the human condition. While his worlds are populated with demons and devils, spirits and monsters, aliens and alternate dimensions, there are human stories. These are worlds you can *believe in* because they resemble our own so acutely. These are not stories from far-off places, nor are these characters foreign: they are people like us, living in places very much like our own, experiencing their hurts and struggles and betrayals with such visceral force it takes your breath away. Despite the monsters, these are stories that we can relate to—and in some ways, that's the most horrifying thing of all.

I think what really appeals to me about these stories is how seamlessly Langan weaves the fantastic with the mundane, the extraordinary with the domestic. These are stories about ordinary people experiencing every day heartache—making them all the more compelling because they could have happened to you or me, to our loved ones, our families and lovers. These are our stories, humanity's stories of all the terrible ways we can damage one another, physically and emotionally. And while the complex emotional arcs alone are enough to propel the story, the demons and monsters and other oddities add layers of nuance and depth and richness to the storytelling, giving body to the human experiences of grief and betrayal and shame.

This exquisite collection is one that begs to be both devoured and savored. The stories provide a thrill that demands sleeping with the light on, lest whatever's been hiding in the dark is free to roam. But they also gnaw at your heartstrings with agonizing relatability. Worse than the creeping dread is the terrible sensation of recognition: these are stories you know—they are *yours*—and yet they are also completely fresh and new. It is this blend of the familiar with the unimaginable that makes reading these stories such a terrible treat. Waiting for you between the pages of this book are painfully familiar scenarios—and nightmares you can't even begin to fathom. Give in to the seduction these pages offer, but beware: betrayal lurks at every turn, and it will consume you.

US (2019)
A GEHENNA POST REVIEW

 couple years back, Jordan Peele blessed us with the film that was *Get Out*, a mindboggling study in cultural stereotypes with a large mix of horror spread throughout. Many were eager to see Peele's sophomoric film *US* for obvious reasons. While it is an entirely different film than *Get Out* in just about every way, it was nonetheless an exhilarating ride through hell. From immense performances from the entire cast to an interesting spin on a classic horror trope of doppelgangers, *US* did not disappoint.

There are still moments of Peele's social commentary in *US* though they are not nearly as direct as in *Get Out*. We follow a family as they navigate the aftermath of an attack from duplicate beings that resemble themselves and everyone around them perfectly. In some ways, it's been compared to *Invasion of the Body Snatchers*, but we didn't find that comparison to do the film justice. For these entities are entirely different beings that can live independently from their *mirrors*, so to speak. Not just that, but they also have a much deeper connection to our protagonists than merely a means of attaining hosts.

The film quickly spirals into very weird territory, abandoning straightforward horror and embracing a cocktail of surrealism and psychological horror. There are many hilarious moments to break the tension, primarily from actor Winston Duke who plays the confused father attempting to understand what is happening all around them. Both child actors, Shahadi Wright Joseph and Evan Alex, are extraordinary in their dual roles. The true shining star, however, is Lupita Nyong'o, whose performance is heartbreaking and chilling. She is at times graceful, kind, and then at other times horrific and unhinged.

There are several twists throughout the film, some handled better than others. We'd encourage potential viewers to go into the film with zero expectations, as these twists could either dampen your experience or possibly heighten it. The cinematography is gorgeous in every shot and the score by Michael Abels is sure to become a classic among horror aficionados. It would be impossible to truly delve into this film without approaching certain spoiler territory, but what we can say is that if viewers who enjoyed *Get Out* wished to see a larger scale, stranger premise that spun the thread of weird fiction with the now famous Peele social commentary, *US* just might satiate your appetite.

CONTRIBUTORS:

INTERVIEWEE:
Max Booth III *is the Editor-in-Chief of Perpetual Motion Machine, the Managing Editor of Dark Moon Digest, and the co-host of Castle Rock Radio, a Stephen King podcast. He's the author of many novels and frequently contributes articles to both LitReactor and CrimeReads. Follow him on Twitter @GiveMeYourTeeth or visit him at http://www.TalesFromTheBooth.com. He lives in Texas.*

AUTHORS:
Ben Thomas is the author of the novel *The Cradle and the Sword*, as well as numerous weird tales, articles and essays. He serves as editor of the history and culture site *The Strange Continent*, and has traveled and lived in more than 40 countries.

Samantha Bryant is a middle school Spanish teacher by day and a novelist by night. That makes her a superhero all the time. Her secret superpower is finding lost things. She writes because it's cheaper than therapy and a lot more fun. She's best known for her *Menopausal Superhero* series of novels and stories.

Lena Ng is from Toronto, Ontario. Her 2018-19 publications include: *Polar Borealis*, *Spectacle*, *Enchanted Conversation*, *ARTPOST*, *NonBinary Review*, *Amazing Stories*, *Zooscape*, *Hinnom*, and the anthologies *We Shall Be Monsters* and *Colp*. "Under an Autumn Moon" is her short story collection. She is currently seeking a publisher for her novel, *Darkness Beckons*, a Gothic romance.

POETS:
Scott J. Couturier is a writer of the Weird, grotesque, perverse, & darkly fantastic. His poetry & prose began cropping up in literary journals & anthologies in 2017 – venues he has contributed to include *The Audient Void*, *Spectral Realms*, *Hinnom Magazine,* & *Weirdbook* (forthcoming). His fiction has been repeatedly featured in the *Test Patterns* & *Pulps* anthologies from Planet X Publications. In 2014, he self-published two dark/Weird fantasy-dystopia novels (first two in a projected five-part series titled *The Magistricide*). 2017 saw publication of the third volume (*The Curse of Roc-Thalian*): the series is currently undergoing edits & evaluation for a future re-release.

Marge Simon lives in Ocala FL. Her fiction and/or poetry has appeared in Asimov's, Daily Science Fiction, Bete Noire, New Myths, and Polu Texni. Her works may be found in anthologies such as Tales of the Lake 5, Chiral Mad 4, You, Human and The Beauty of Death. Marge has won the Bram Stoker Award, the Rhysling, Elgin, Dwarf Stars and Strange Horizons Readers' Awards; she serves on the HWA Board of Trustees, maintains a newsletter column, Blood & Spades. Marge is the second woman to be acknowledged as a Grand Master Poet of the SFPA, and is on the board of the Speculative Literary Foundation. She attends the ICFA annually as a guest. www.margesimon.com

Alessandro Manzetti (Rome, Italy) is a Bram Stoker Award-winning (and 7-time nominee) author, editor, and translator of horror fiction and dark poetry whose work has been published extensively in Italian, including novels, short and long fiction, poetry, essays, and collections.

GUEST COLUMN:
Melissa Burkley received her Ph.D. in psychology from the University of North Carolina at Chapel Hill. As a professor, she has conducted hundreds of scientific studies and her work has been featured in *The New York Times*, *Cosmopolitan*, and *Oprah Radio*. As a writer, her work has appeared in the 2017 *Women in Horror Annual* and *The Psychology of Dexter*, *Girl with the Dragon Tattoo*, and *Twilight* books. Her blog, entitled "The Writer's Laboratory," teaches authors how to improve their writing by incorporating psychological principles into their work. She writes a second blog for *Psychology Today* called "The Social Thinker." Because of her dual-expertise in psychology and storytelling, she is frequently sought after by film companies who want a psychological analysis of their movies and characters (e.g., *Blood Honey*, *Lovesick Fool*). Visit her website at www.melissaburkley.com

REVIEWER:
Lisa Quigley is first and foremost passionately devoted to the craft of horror and weird fiction. Last year, she had two fiction publications: "Redemption" in *Automata Review* and "Birth" in the November issue of *Unnerving Magazine*—a special Stephen King themed issue. For three years, she was a contributing writer on the blog *Dwarf + Giant*, where she reviewed books and interviewed authors. Some of her favorites over there are: a review of Paul Tremblay's Disappearance at Devil's Rock, an interview with Paul Tremblay, and a contribution to a special

Halloween series initiated by The Last Bookstore. Currently, she is the Creative Director and co-host of a dark fiction podcast called *Ladies of the Fright* (http://www.ladiesofthefright.com.) In a former life, she was the Editorial Assistant for *IDEA Fitness Journal,* where she gained real-world editorial experience and knowledge of the periodical publishing industry. She also researched and wrote the Buzz, Member Spotlight, and Product Showcase for *IFJ*, in addition to the occasional feature article.

ILLUSTRATORS:
Dave Dick – Cover Art
Sean O'Keefe – Interior Illustrations
David Dawkins – Interior Illustrations

EDITORS:
C. P. Dunphey is a Staten Island-born expat dwelling in the dirty south, and is perhaps best known for his novel Plane Walker and as the founder/editor-in-chief of Gehenna & Hinnom Books. Along with editing Hinnom Magazine and anthologies like the Year's Best Body Horror and the upcoming Year's Best Cosmic Horror, his work has appeared and/or is forthcoming in publications such as Weirdbook and the anthologies 1816: The Year Without Summer - Unredacted Cthulhu Almanac and 32 White Horses on a Vermillion Hill.

Caleb Stephens is a CPA and author who resides in Denver, Colorado. His short stories have been published in *Horror Tales Podcast, Ink Stains,* and *Hinnom Magazine*, for which he is the Assistant Editor. His stories have also received honorable mentions in *Writer's Digest* and *Allegory Magazine*. He is currently neck deep in his second novel, a dark speculative horror thriller that keeps him up way too late at night. When he's not writing, he can be found honing his guitar chops or playing with his three daughters. Learn more about his work at www.calebstephensauthor.com and follow him on Twitter and Medium @cstephensauthor.

SUPPORTER OF THIS ISSUE VIA PATREON!

Candace Nola

MAX BOOTH III

ORDER ON AMAZON TODAY!

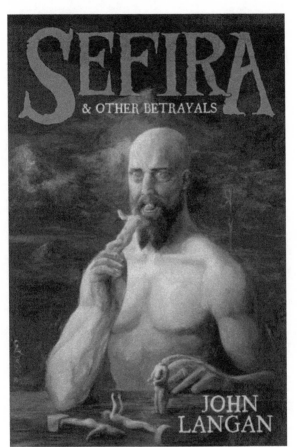

GEHENNA & HINNOM BOOKS

FACEBOOK:
https://www.facebook.com/gehennaandhinnombooks/

TWITTER:
https://twitter.com/gehennabooks

INSTAGRAM:
https://www.instagram.com/gehennabooks/

WEBSITE:
https://gehennabooks.com/

PATREON:
https://www.patreon.com/gehennabooks

If you enjoyed this book, please leave a review on Amazon and Goodreads!

CPSIA information can be obtained
at www.ICGtesting.com
Printed in the USA
FFHW020603221119
56109906-62188FF

9 781950 642021